For Ferre, Warre, Loren, and tiny Wiebelmie.
— *S. v. M.*

Especially for Lev, Victor, Jarne, and Marie.
Thank you Fien, Onas, and Lev.
— *C. W.*

Original title: *Mina Lieverd*
© 2010 by Uitgeverij De Eenhoorn, Vlasstraat 17, B-8710 Wielsbeke, Belgium
Text © Sine van Mol
Illustrations © Carianne Wijffels

This edition published in 2011 by
Eerdmans Books for Young Readers,
an imprint of
Wm. B. Eerdmans Publishing Co.
2140 Oak Industrial Dr. NE, Grand Rapids, Michigan 49505
P.O. Box 163, Cambridge CB3 9PU U.K.

www.eerdmans.com/youngreaders

Manufactured at Tien Wah Press, in Singapore, March 2011, first edition

17 16 15 14 13 12 11   8 7 6 5 4 3 2 1

Library of Congress Cataloging-in-Publication Data

Mol, Sine van.
[Mina lieverd. English]
Meena / by Sine van Mol; illustrated by Carianne Wijffels.
p. cm.
Summary: The children of Fly Street fear and taunt their neighbor Meena, thinking she is a witch,
but when they meet her granddaughter and taste her red cherry pie, they learn the truth.
ISBN 978-0-8028-5394-3 (alk. paper)
[1. Old age — Fiction. 2. Grandmothers — Fiction. 3. Prejudices — Fiction. 4. Fear — Fiction.]
I. Wijffels, Carianne, ill. II. Title.
PZ7.M7314Dar 2011
[E] — dc22
2010049547

Meena

Sine van Mol   illustrated by Carianne Wijffels

Eerdmans Books for Young Readers

Grand Rapids, Michigan • Cambridge, U.K.

The children of Fly Street were afraid of Meena.

"Meena is a witch," Christa declared.
"She eats toads," Klaas shouted.
"She drinks blood," Thomas added.

From a safe place, at a safe distance, they shouted,
    "Fa-at Mee-na, Fa-at Mee-na,
    catch us if you can!"

Sometimes they came a little closer, their hearts pounding.
They sang faster and faster. Louder and louder.

Then they ran away.

Meena couldn't catch them anyway. They knew that.
But as soon as they heard clatter from behind the front door,
        Klaas, Thomas, and Christa rushed away.

Then one day they saw something horrible.
Or so they thought.
"Look!" Klaas shouted. "Fat Meena has a little girl at her house!"
"Imprisoned . . ." Thomas stammered.
"Next time it's our turn," Christa shivered.
Never had they been so afraid.

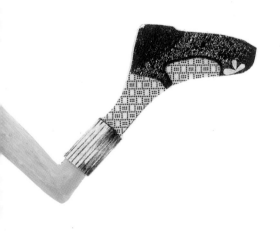

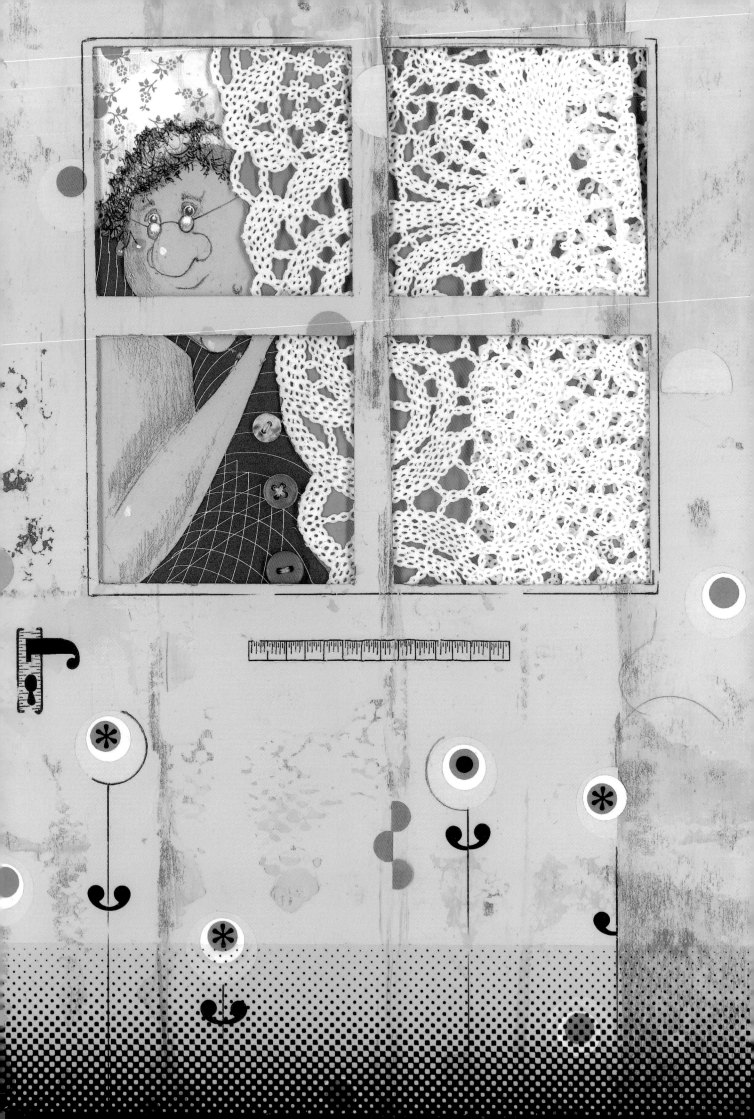

"We could throw her in prison," Klaas said.

"We could push her in the oven," Christa suggested.

"We could knock down her whole house," Thomas added.

With chalk they wrote WITCH on the street, with an arrow
    pointing to Meena's house.

"Now everybody will know," Christa said.

"Now she'll have to move," Klaas and Thomas agreed.

But Meena didn't move.

The girl was still alive.

She came to visit Meena often.

She played near the wall and sometimes
    she walked down the street.

"W-I-T-C-H," she spelled.

She turned her head in the direction of the arrow.

She saw Klaas, Thomas, and Christa.

"Come here!" they shouted. "We've got to tell you something!"

"Who are you?" Christa asked.

"My name is Anna," the girl replied.

"Did she put a spell on you?" Klaas asked.

"Who?" Anna looked at them with surprise.

"The witch. Did the witch put a spell on you
so that now you have to visit her all the time?"

"She's not a witch! She's my grandma."
Anna looked at them angrily.
"But she eats little children. Does she have a wart . . . ?"
"MY. GRANDMA. IS. NOT. A. WITCH!" Anna roared,
        and she ran inside.
"Completely under a spell," Klaas sighed.
"Horrible," Christa shivered.
"There she is!" Klaas shouted when Meena came outside.
She emptied a bucket into the gutter.

"A bucket full of blood," Christa shuddered.
"It makes her hands completely red . . ." Klaas shivered.
"Watch out, Anna!" Christa shouted.
But Anna didn't listen.

"This witch has to go," Christa declared.

"Let's send her a letter," Thomas said.

"With poison. So she will drop dead," Klaas suggested.

"She has to go away, not die," Thomas argued.

He wrote on a piece of paper:

      GO AWAY OR ELSE!!!!

"Next we throw this letter over the wall," Thomas said.

"You throw it and we'll stand guard," Christa said.

Thomas crept closer and closer.

The fear crawled from his toes up to his legs.

His heart was pounding. He could barely breathe.

I dare, don't dare, dare . . . was going through his head.

He was standing next to the wall.

He could hear Anna and Meena talking and laughing.

He stretched his arm and threw the letter . . .

Meena caught the letter and looked over the wall.
"Hi," she said.
Thomas stood as if pinned to the ground.

Meena unfolded the letter and read it. A deep wrinkle
        appeared on her forehead. She looked at Thomas.
"Are you so afraid, child?" she asked.
Her voice sounded friendly. Thomas slowly exhaled.
"There is nothing to be afraid of," Anna said,
        and she gave her grandma a kiss.

"Grandma baked a pie," Anna said. "You want a piece?"
"No thanks," Thomas whispered.
"You don't even dare to taste the most delicious pie in the world.
        I feel sorry for you," Anna said, and took a big bite.
"Toa…toad-blood pie," Thomas stammered. In a moment Anna
        would drop dead.
"Are you crazy?" Anna shouted. "Cherry pie."

"Taste it," Meena encouraged him.
With the tip of his tongue he touched
    a piece of the pie. Delicious.
"Grandma does have a wart,
    but not on her nose," Anna grinned.
Cautiously Thomas took a bite, and another one,
    and another one and another one.

Anna called Christa and Klaas.
They tiptoed forward.
"Cherry pie. Delicious," Thomas told them.
Klaas took a piece, but Christa ran away.

Tomorrow my friends will be dead, she thought.
Stone dead.
That night she had horrible dreams.

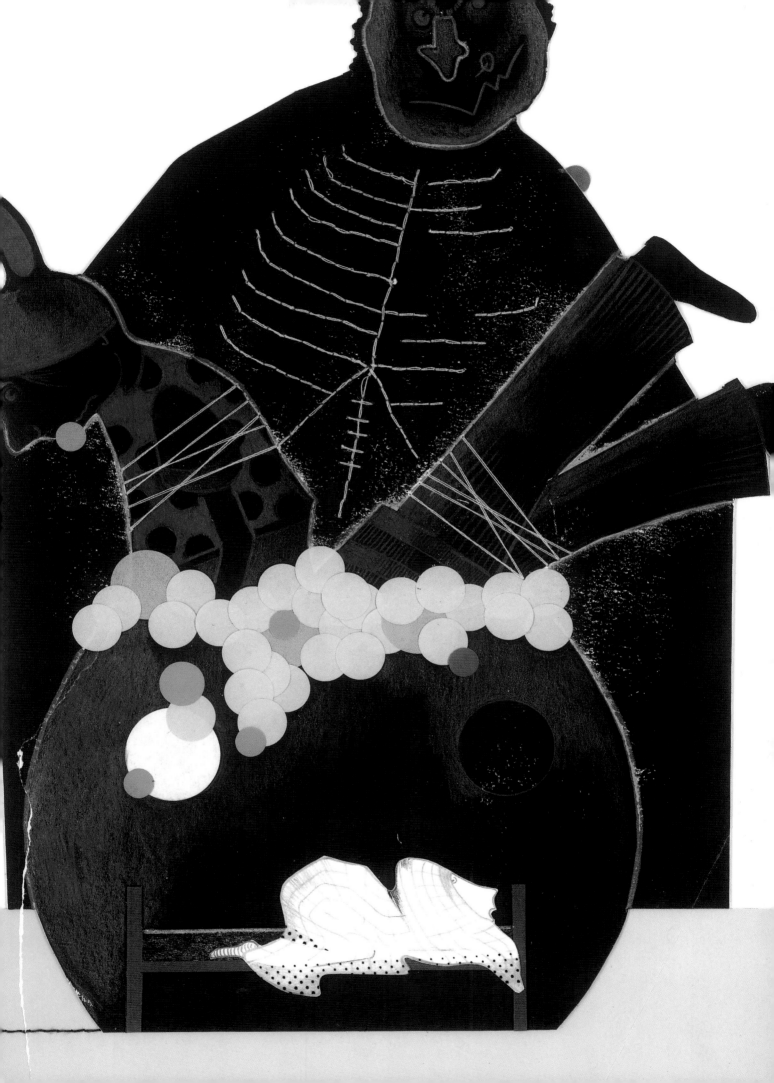

The next day Thomas and Klaas were alive and kicking.

"Come on," Christa called, relieved.

"Where to?" the boys asked.

"To Grandma Meena's!" Christa shouted.

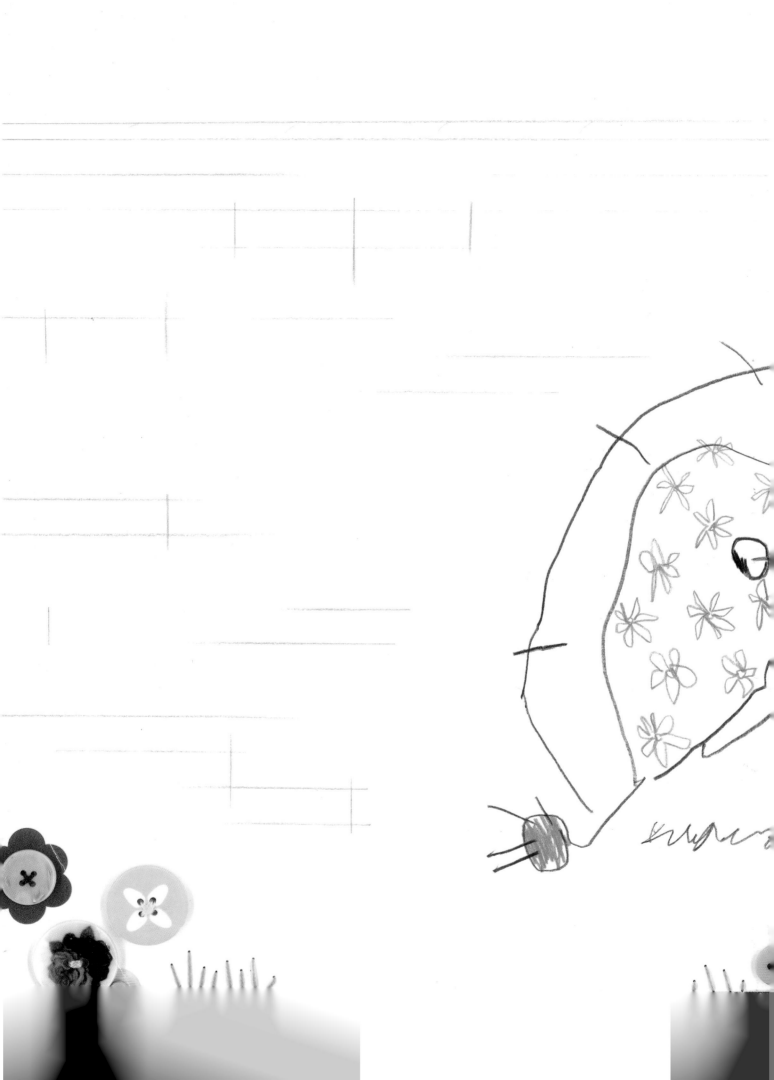